ADVENTURES IN THE KINGDOM™

SEEKER'S GREAT ADVENTURE

Written by Dian Layton.
Illustrations created by Al Berg.

FROM THE PAGES OF
THE GREAT BOOK

The people who KNOW their King
shall have mega-muscles inside
and go on great ADVENTURES!
Daniel 11:32b Yeah!

(From the Hugga-Wugga™ Paraphrase H.W.P.)

Illustrations created by Al Berg.

Published by MercyPlace Ministries

Distributed by

Destiny Image® Publishers, Inc.
P.O. Box 310
Shippensburg, PA 17257-0310

ISBN 0-9677402-1-5

For Worldwide Distribution
Printed in the U.S.A.

This book and all other Destiny Image, Revival Press, MercyPlace, Fresh Bread, and Treasure House books are available at Christian bookstores and distributors worldwide.

For a U.S. bookstore nearest you, call **1-800-722-6774**.
For more information on foreign distributors, call **717-532-3040**.
Or reach us on the Internet: **http://www.reapernet.com**

CONTENTS

Glee

Gladness

Giggles

Seeker

Dawdle

Slow

Doodle

Do

Yes

HopeSo

KnowSo

To Seekers everywhere...

May you Really Know the King

and have great adventures

in His Kingdom!

Seeker

CHAPTER ONE

Seeker opened his window and took a deep breath of the fresh morning air. *Perfect!* he thought. *I can't wait to get on the roller coaster again today!*

With both hands cupped under his chin, Seeker dreamily looked out his window. In the distance he could see the flags at the CARNALville of Selfishness waving brightly. Yesterday, like so many other days, Seeker and his friends had spent most of their time at the CARNALville, thinking only about themselves. (Going to a carnival isn't wrong; but going to the CARNALville of Selfishness is *very* wrong!)

The clowns at the CARNALville had introduced a new roller coaster yesterday

1

and encouraged the children to ride it as many times as they wanted. Plus there were huge free samples of candy. The CARNALville candy was made from the clowns' own special secret recipe. It was all so delicious that the more the children ate, the more they wanted to eat. At night, even though their stomachs ached, all they could think of was going again the next day to the CARNVALville to eat more candy.

Thinking about the candy made Seeker's mouth water. He licked his lips and closed his eyes for a long time. Suddenly, Seeker's daydream was interrupted by his mother's voice. "Seeker! It's almost time to leave for the King's Celebration. Are you ready?"

The King's Celebration...oh no! Seeker had forgotten all about the King's Celebration. It was a special day each week of fun and laughter and good food in the Grand Throne Room. The King's minstrels played their instruments and sang new songs for the King. The castle servants served the best meals that anyone had ever tasted; and the King's friend Jester-Minute played games and told stories. Jester-Minute made the people laugh so hard that tears rolled down their faces and washed away any sadness that might have been hiding in their hearts.

But there was one very surprising problem about the Celebration. The children didn't like it. The children didn't like it at all. The more time they spent at Selfishness, the more restless they became at the Celebration, and the more grouchy and disobedient they became at home. Because the only thing that really mattered to the children of the Kingdom was themselves.

2

Seeker's mother called out to him again, "Are you ready, Seeker?"

Seeker sighed, "Well, I guess I can just forget about the candy and the roller coaster for today."

He reached in the closet for his Celebration clothes and slammed the door.

Seeker was grouchy and quiet as he walked with his mother, Contentment, and his older sister, Moira, through the village streets. When they reached the big rock at the base of the Straight and Narrow Path, Seeker couldn't bear it any longer. He stopped and pleaded with Contentment, "Mom! Do I *have* to go to the King's Celebration?"

Contentment tried to control her surprise. She cleared her throat and said, "Moira, you go on ahead. Your brother and I need to have a little talk." When Moira was well on her way up the path, Contentment turned to her son. "Seeker! You know very well that we go to the King's Celebration every week. We've been going every single week for years—ever since the King brought us out of the Village of Fear into his Kingdom. What's the matter with you?"

"I want to go to the CARNALville today," Seeker whined.

"It seems to me that you have been spending far too much time at that CARNALville lately, Seeker!"

3

"But Mom! The King's Celebration is *boring!*"

Contentment shook her head sadly. "Oh, Seeker, if only you would get to *know* the King, then you would *love* going to his Celebration." Contentment sighed a deep sigh and turned back toward the Straight and Narrow Path. "Come on."

Seeker and his mother walked up the path. The beautiful white castle with its golden trim sparkled in the sunlight. The Royal Doorkeeper stood waiting at the great front door to welcome the villagers from Peace and Harmony. He smiled at Seeker and Contentment as they entered the castle and walked down the shining hallway toward the King's Grand Throne Room.

At night, Seeker had dreams about that hallway.

He dreamed of taking off his shoes and sliding from one end right down to the other end. Sometimes he dreamed that he and the other children slid together. And sometimes, he even dreamed of being able to explore the castle. He wondered if there were other shining hallways, and he wondered what was inside the castle towers.

Seeker looked up and realized that his mother was far ahead of him, waiting impatiently at the entrance to the Grand Throne Room. As Seeker hurried to catch up, his feet gave just a hint of a slide on the shining hallway floor.

4

CHAPTER TWO

Three great tables were set and ready for the King's Celebration. As Seeker and Contentment entered the Grand Throne Room and sat down at a banquet table, Seeker waved to his friends. Seeker's friends were very interesting and unusual children. HopeSo, KnowSo, and Yes were always confident and outgoing. Giggles, Gladness, and Glee loved to have fun. Dawdle and Slow talked and walked together very slowly. Doodle and Do were always discussing about which one of them would get to do something.

The King's acrobats and jugglers ran into the room, performing cartwheels and somersaults across the floor. Jester-Minute passed out long ribbons and streamers to the villagers and the Celebration began. The villagers stood to their feet

9

as dozens of minstrels began to make music for the King. Some people clapped, some danced, some waved banners and flags. Laughter and music filled the Grand Throne Room and poured out into the world beyond the Kingdom, bringing hope to everyone who would pause and turn their ears to listen.

Then the castle servants brought in golden trays of food that were served to the villagers on glass plates (that wouldn't break if you accidentally dropped one). Delicious smells filled the air. There were platters of roasted meats, vegetables and fruits of every kind, and warm breads fresh from the royal ovens. The dessert trays were set up for everyone to help themselves whenever they wanted—because the Celebration desserts weren't just good to eat, they were also good for eating! Every food at the King's banquet made his people healthy and strong. The villagers stopped dancing for now, and sat down at the tables, continuing to laugh and sing as they enjoyed the meal. Everyone was happy. Everyone, that is, but Seeker.

"This is so boring!" he mumbled to himself. "All you do here is sing, sing, sing! And it's all the King's fault!"

Seeker looked angrily toward the throne, but what he saw there took him completely by surprise. The King, who was usually smiling and friendly, was not smiling. The King, who usually sang along with his people, was not singing. Instead, the great King of Joy and Peace was very, very sad. Seeker had never ever seen such sadness on anyone's face, and the anger he had been feeling inside quickly disappeared. In its place was a deep concern for the King. Seeker was worried.

The music and laughter of the Celebration faded into the background as Seeker watched the King. Why was the King sad? Didn't anyone care? How could the villagers sing so loudly when the King felt like that? Didn't anyone notice that the King wasn't singing with them today? Seeker tugged at his mother. "Mom, look at the King. Why is he so sad?" Contentment looked up from her meal. "Hmmm? I don't know, Seeker; now eat your food."

"But Mom, just look at him! Something is wrong. Why isn't the King singing with us today?"

Contentment put a finger to her lips and whispered, "I don't know why the King is sad, Seeker! Just be content and enjoy the banquet!" Then Contentment saw the hurt look in Seeker's eyes. "Don't worry, Seeker," she said. "If something is bothering the King, he will take care of it."

Seeker started to nibble at his meal, but he couldn't stop thinking about the King. He looked back toward the throne. It just didn't make sense! There, surrounded by the laughter and singing of his people, the King was sad. Why? Then Seeker realized that the King was looking at the third banquet table. Villagers from Peace and Harmony filled every seat at the other two tables, but the third table was empty. It was filled with food, but no one was there to enjoy it. While Seeker wondered about that, the most amazing thing happened.

Suddenly the King turned, looked right at Seeker, leaned forward, and winked at him!

11

Seeker's eyes grew big with surprise. He tugged hard at his mother. "Mom! The King! He winked at me!"

"Oh? That's nice, Seeker. Now eat your food."

"But Mom! The King winked at me! He actually winked at me!" A finger to her lips and a glance from his mother made Seeker turn back to his meal. He munched quietly for a few moments. Then, ever so carefully, he turned his eyes again toward the King. A wave of delighted surprise washed over him. The King was still looking right at him! When Seeker's eyes met his, the King leaned forward and winked again.

"Mom! The King! He winked at me *again!*"

"That's *nice*, Seeker. *Eat...your...food.*"

Seeker ate his food, but he kept looking at the King. The King looked at Seeker; Seeker looked at the King; and something started to happen in Seeker's heart.

CHAPTER THREE

That night, as Seeker got ready for bed and Contentment came to tuck him in, he said, "Mom, will you tell me again what the King did for us? I mean, tell me about where we used to live."

Contentment sat down, remembering. "Fear," she said with a shiver. "We lived in Fear—all the time, every day. It was so awful, Seeker. I'm glad you were just a baby, and you don't remember those days. You don't remember the dragon..."

Seeker sat up. "Oh yeah. Tell me again about the dragon."

Contentment shuddered. "Ugly, horrible, slimy, smelly. He had the most disgusting habit of picking his nose and burping out loud—just to be rude. The dragon used to breathe thoughts into our minds continually—thoughts about being afraid... afraid of everything."

"Afraid of everything?" Seeker echoed.

Contentment nodded sadly. "We were afraid to go outside, but even more afraid to stay inside. We were afraid of people, but more afraid to be alone. We were afraid of the dark, afraid of the light. We were afraid of everything! All the time, every day...we lived in Fear."

Contentment seemed lost in the horrible memories. Seeker gently called to her, "But Mom...Mom...the King changed all that, right?"

Contentment smiled, "Yes, Seeker, the King changed all that. He set us free from Fear. One day, he marched right into the village, looked the dragon right in the eye, and began to sing!"

"Sing?" Seeker echoed in surprise. He didn't remember hearing this part of the story before!

His mother nodded, "That was a strange thing to do to a dragon, don't you think? But it worked! The King sang about not being afraid, about trusting and believing. And as he sang, the dragon became smaller and smaller and smaller, until it disappeared!"

"Wow!" Seeker exclaimed.

"Then the King brought all of us who had lived in Fear into the Village of Peace and Harmony here in his Kingdom." Contentment continued, "And he taught us a song to sing if ever the Dragon Fear tried to make us afraid again. It went like this…"

Oooky-pooky-spooky fear,
You have no right to come near!
In the King's name, you get out of here;
Fear, be gone, be gone!
Fear, be gone!

Seeker was impressed. " 'In the King's name, you get out of here.' Wow. If you say that, then the Dragon Fear goes away?"

His mother nodded, "If you say that, then any dragon has to go away. The King's name is like a powerful weapon and when you use his name against dragons, they know they are in big trouble!"

Contentment put her arm around Seeker's shoulders. "Seeker, I'm so glad we talked about all this. I needed to remember what the King did for us. I've been far too content with life here in Peace and Harmony. I need to be more of a *seeker*!"

Seeker smiled back at his mother. Then he paused and said, "Mom, remember how the King winked at me today at the Celebration? Well, I've been thinking, and well, uh, can I get to know and love the King, like you do?"

"Oh, yes, Seeker!" Contentment responded, "as long as you *really* want to! That is very, very important. People can live in the Kingdom...they can eat at the King's banquet table every week...but no one actually gets to *know* the King unless they *really* want to."

Contentment pulled back slightly and looked Seeker in the eye. "Do you *really* want to?"

"Uh-huh," Seeker nodded solemnly.

To his amazement, Contentment shook her head and folded her arms firmly. "No. You must *really* want to! Do you *really* want to, Seeker?"

Seeker thought. He thought about his friends. He thought about the CARNALville of Selfishness. He thought about the clowns, and the rides, and the candy. And then Seeker thought about how the King had looked at him, and suddenly, none of those other things mattered at all. "Yes," he said with confidence. "Yes, I *really* want to!"

"All right!" Contentment smiled as she stood to her feet. "Then you can go tomorrow...to see the King...all by yourself!"

"Tomorrow?" Seeker was surprised. "To see the King? All by myself?"

"All by yourself," Contentment repeated, tucking him under the covers on his bed. "Goodnight, Seeker. Sweet dreams." She put out the lamp and closed the door quietly behind her.

"Wow!" Seeker said to himself, "All by myself to see the King! What am I going to say? What is he going to say? What are we going to say? Hmm...I better practice. Let's see...

"I should be very *official*, stand and say, 'Good *day*, Your *Majesty*.'

"Or... maybe I should be more *friendly* and say, '*Hello*, your *Majesty*.'

17

"Hmm... or maybe..." Seeker's eyes twinkled, "I should have *fun* and say, 'Hey, Your Majesty! What's happenin'?!'

Seeker laughed and then shook his head. "But no, that's not the right way to talk to the King. I'll say, 'Good day, your majesty!' That's the best (yawn) Just think, yesterday all I wanted to do was go to the CARNALville, but now... (yawn) I want to know... the King."

Seeker fell asleep. He dreamed all night about the King and the castle with the long shining hallways.

CHAPTER FOUR

The next morning, when the rooster crowed, Seeker jumped out of bed, got dressed, ran downstairs, ate his breakfast, and headed toward the door. His mother was standing there, smiling and holding his toothbrush. "Oops! Forgot about my teeth!" Seeker instantly brushed his teeth and gave his mother a quick hug. "Bye, Mom! I'm going to see the King!"

"All by yourself," Contentment said with a smile.

Seeker ran through the streets of Peace and Harmony toward the castle. But then, the closer he got to the Straight and Narrow Path, the less confident Seeker began to feel. He slowed down to a walk.

"I'm going to see the King," he gulped and walked even more slowly. "*All by myself?*"

He stood at the big rock at the base of the hill and looked up at the castle. "Wow. The Straight and Narrow Path never used to look so straight, and so narrow," he said, looking at it from different angles. "Well, I'd better practice what I'm going to say. Let's see...'Good day, Your Majesty. Good *day*, Your *Majesty*!'" Seeker straightened his shoulders and took a deep breath. "Okay, here I go!"

He was just about to start up the path when suddenly, he heard the voices of his friends, HopeSo, KnowSo, and Yes; Giggles, Gladness, and Glee; Dawdle and Slow; and Doodle and Do. As usual, Seeker's friends were with some of the CARNALville clowns. They all came running toward him, happily singing their song...

CARNALville! CARNALville! We love to go
To the CARNALville all day long!
Up and down, round and round,
Merrily go around,
We love the CARNALville so!

As long as he could remember, Seeker and the other children had sung that song. It was a happy, catchy little tune. It seemed so much fun to have all the candy and fun they wanted; but if any child had ever paused to look, or if they had stopped to really think about how selfish they were acting, they would have seen beyond the cheerful clown masks. They would have seen right through the disguise to some very wicked dragons hiding underneath the innocent-looking clown costumes. And, they would have realized that the CARNALville clowns sang another song when the children weren't listening. It was a nasty little song:

> *This is the CARNALville of Selfishness*
> *And we've got a hold of the Kingdom's Kids.*
> *Aha, ha ha ha;Aha ha aha ha ha ha.*
> *Aha ha aha ha ha ha.*

Today the clowns whispered among themselves and picked their noses nervously as they watched the village children run toward Seeker. (The dragons found it quite difficult to pick their noses while wearing the clown masks, but they couldn't seem to stop. It was just one of their gross and disgusting habits.)

Giggles called out happily, "Hi, Seeker. C'mon! We're going to the CARNALville!"

"A-a-are you c-c-coming, S-S-Seeker?" Dawdle and Slow asked together.

"Well, I should hope so!" HopeSo exclaimed.

"I know so!" said KnowSo.

"Yes, yes, of course he is!" Yes nodded vigorously.

Seeker answered a bit timidly, "Well, no. Actually, I'm not! I'm *not* going to the CARNALville today."

21

"*What?!*" his friends cried in amazement.

"*What?!*" the clowns cried with equal amazement. They had been listening quietly, but now sprang into action. They pulled out their CARNALville balloons and

candy, made sure their masks were in place, and hurried closer to the children. "Here is some yummy, yummy candy for you, kids," they smiled. "And remember, there's more and more and more candy waiting for you at the CARNALville today!"

The children grabbed handfuls of candy and stuffed their mouths full. But Seeker shook his head and pushed the clowns away. "I don't want any of your candy!" he said firmly. The clowns and the children were even more amazed. "No candy?" they cried.

"Wh-wh-what's wrong, S-S-Seeker?" Dawdle and Slow stuttered. "Are you s-s-sick or s-s-something?"

"Yes!" Seeker felt courage fill his heart. "I'm sick of that CARNALville! Sometimes those rides make my head hurt! And sometimes my stomach feels sick!"

The children responded, "But the candy tastes dandy. We don't think there can be anything better than it!"

Seeker squared his shoulders and responded, "Well, I think there could be! And I want to find out! I'm going to see the King...all by myself!"

"You're *what?!*" the children cried in amazement.

"You're *what?!*" the clowns echoed. At the very mention of the King, their bodies began to tremble and they started to nervously pick their noses (which was quite difficult to do while wearing a mask).

Dawdle and Slow spoke up again, "C-c-c'mon, S-S-Seeker! We j-j-just had to go to that b-b-boring c-c-celebration yesterday!"

"Yeah!" HopeSo agreed. "C'mon, Seeker! What's wrong with you?"

"Nothing's wrong with *me!*" Seeker tried to explain. "I'm just starting to realize that the Kingdom is better than the CARNALville—and I'm going to see the King!" Seeker turned away from his friends, away from the CARNALville clowns, and started toward the castle once again.

24

But then, from beside the path, one of the clowns stuck his foot in the way and tripped Seeker, making him fall down! The clown pretended to be surprised, "Oh, you poor thing! What a nasty fall! Why don't you just sit down over here and have a bit of candy to help you feel better." The clown motioned to another clown who quickly offered Seeker some especially tasty candy.

"I don't want your candy!" he cried, pushing the candy away. As Seeker pushed, the clown was caught off balance and fell backwards onto the ground. As he fell, the clown mask shifted over to one side. Seeker saw the dark and slimy ugliness underneath the mask before the clown quickly set it back onto his face.

"Dragon!" Seeker shouted. "You aren't a clown at all. You're a dragon!" Seeker turned toward the other clown. "You!" Seeker cried. "You are another dragon!"

The children had huddled together, surprised by Seeker's burst of anger. Giggles was the first to speak. "Seeker," she giggled nervously, "you must have hit your head really hard when you fell! Are you all right?"

Glee laughed, "Seeker, come on. There aren't any dragons this close to the Kingdom! These are just clowns. That's all, just clowns."

The clowns waved and spoke in candy-coated voices. "That's right, boys and girls, we're just sweet little clowns!"

Seeker shook his head. "Dragons," he repeated. "They are dragons, and all you kids better get away from them!"

Gladness took one of the clowns by the hand and laughed. "Look at me, everybody! I'm holding on to a really bad dragon! I'm sure *glad* it doesn't bite!" The clown licked a lollipop innocently and the other children laughed.

"L-L-Let's get g-g-going to the CARNALville," Dawdle and Slow said together.

"Yes!" agreed Yes with a flip of her curls. "Let's leave Seeker alone. He needs to get busy. Maybe there are more dragons hiding around here for him to find!" Yes pretended to pick her nose and search for dragons. The other children laughed and began to pick their noses also, while making fun of Seeker.

"It's not funny," he whispered, biting back the tears that threatened to spill out. "The clowns are dragons! You need to be careful!" The children just laughed harder. The clowns made fun of him, and some of the children, even his very best friends, called him names. It hurt Seeker inside, but he turned back toward the Straight and Narrow Path, all by himself. "I don't care what you call me!" Seeker said, wiping away the tears that escaped from his eyes. "I'm going to see the King!" He began to run up the path toward the castle.

From the bottom of the hill, the clowns and children tried again to stop him. "The King is boring, Seeker!" they called. "Come with us to the CARNALville!" "We have candy for you, Seeker," called the clowns. "Lots and lots of candy!" As Seeker ran, the clowns and children continued to call out to him. He shut out their voices and focused on what he planned to say to the King, "Good day, Your Majesty! Good *day*, Your *Majesty*!" Finally, the clowns and children gave up and went on their way to the CARNALville.

CHAPTER FIVE

When Seeker reached the castle, he saw the Royal Doorkeeper standing in front of the door. It was a huge white door with beautiful gold trim. Above it, written in golden letters, were the words, "Whosoever will may freely come." But Seeker wasn't looking at the words. His eyes were fixed on the Royal Doorkeeper, who seemed to look especially firm and official that day. "Who are you?" the Doorkeeper asked. "And what do you want?"

"My name is Seeker, and I want to see the King," Seeker answered, trying to sound confident.

The Doorkeeper leaned toward him, squinted his eyes in concentration, and spoke with a firm voice, "Do you *really* want to see the King?"

Seeker started to feel less confident. "Uh-huh," he responded hesitantly.

The Doorkeeper shook his head and folded his arms firmly. "No. You must *really* want to! Do you *really* want to?"

Seeker didn't answer right away. He was thinking. He was thinking about how the King had looked at him and how the King had winked at him. Seeker began to feel confident again. He squared his shoulders, took a deep breath, and answered the Royal Doorkeeper, "Yes sir, I really want to see the *King!*"

The Doorkeeper smiled and opened the castle door. "Great! Whosoever will—whoever really wants to—may freely come!" The Doorkeeper led Seeker into the castle.

Seeker's knees were trembling, and he could feel his heart pounding in his chest as he walked down the long shining hallway with the Doorkeeper. No thoughts of sliding came today as Seeker walked on that floor. All he could think of was seeing the King. "Good day, your Majesty. Good *day*, Your *Majesty!*" he practiced quietly.

When they reached the entrance to the Grand Throne Room, the Doorkeeper slowly opened the huge double doors. He bowed to the King and then stretched out his hand toward Seeker, motioning for the boy to enter the

Throne Room. The Doorkeeper then stepped back, and Seeker went, all by himself, into the presence of the King.

Seeker stared at the floor as he slowly walked toward the throne. He had never been in that room before except for the weekly Celebration. Today, there was no laughter and music of the villagers, no happy clanging of dishes of food being passed around. The only sound in the Grand Throne Room was Seeker's beating heart and his footsteps approaching the throne. Finally, he stood before the King, holding his hands together anxiously. A long moment passed. When Seeker finally felt enough courage to look up, he was surprised and relieved to see the King smiling at him. It was a very gentle, happy smile. Seeker smiled back, and then remembered his manners. He knelt down, cleared his throat, took a deep breath, and started to recite his practiced greeting.

"Good d..." Something about the way the King was smiling at him made Seeker stop. He waited just a moment and then, before he had time to think about it, he said, "Hi." The word just came out of Seeker's mouth. He felt embarrassed. Why did he do that? You don't just say, "Hi" to a king! But the King just smiled a bigger smile and said, "Hi."

There was a brief silence, then Seeker looked up again. "My name is Seeker," he said softly.

The King bent closer, looked right into Seeker's eyes, and said just as softly, "I know."

Seeker looked deep into the King's kind eyes and spoke with all his heart, "I *really* want to get to know you."

The King bent closer yet and said with all *his* heart, "I know."

The King reached out his great hands and said, "Come, I will show you my castle!"

"Show me your castle?" Seeker echoed, his eyes getting large and excited. "You mean you will really show me your castle?!"

The King laughed. "Yes! And the first place we will go is right down the shining hallway!" Seeker shyly put his hand into the King's big hand. They walked across the Grand Throne Room and stood together at the end of the shining hallway. The King leaned over and spoke very seriously, "Take off your shoes, Seeker."

Seeker wondered if the King was worried about him scratching the floor or something. Without questioning, he took off his shoes.

To Seeker's utter amazement, the King took off his shoes, too! Then, very seriously but with laughter twinkling from his eyes, the King reached out and took hold of Seeker's hand again.

"Shall we?" said the King, and off they went—sliding down the shining hallway!

This was even better than any dream Seeker had ever dreamed; he had never imagined himself sliding on the shining hallway with the King! Up and down and back and forth they slid. Each time they reached the end, the King would pick Seeker up, twirl him around, and then off they would slide together back to the other end. Finally, they collapsed in the Grand Throne Room, breathless and happy.

After a few moments, the King leapt to his feet and laughed a great laugh. The sound of his laughter echoed past the castle halls, down the hill, and through the streets of Peace and Harmony. Villagers looked up from their work as a delighted shiver briefly overtook them. The King's laughter continued to echo until it reached the CARNALville of Selfishness. Suddenly, the candy the children were eating didn't taste as good as it used to taste, and the rides didn't seem as exciting. The children held their tummies, looked around, and realized that they felt very, very empty inside.

Meanwhile, back at the castle, the King stretched out his hand to Seeker again. "That was fun!" he said. "Let's slide some more!"

The castle servants came and watched the King and Seeker sliding back and forth down the shining hallway. "We've never seen him act like this before!" they said to each other, shaking their heads in amazement. Then the King took Seeker on a tour of the castle. They slid down other shining hallways, climbed up into secret towers, and ran down winding staircases. And they explored some of the deep, mysterious parts of the castle. Seeker's favorite discovery was an underground waterfall. The spray of water on his face felt delicious and alive.

Then the King ordered a royal picnic lunch to be prepared. He and Seeker ate together beside the river at the base of the Straight and Narrow Path. They spent the afternoon there, skipping rocks across the water and fishing. The King explained how water from the Grand Throne Room fountain tumbled down the underground waterfall and flowed out into the river, where everyone in the Kingdom could enjoy the clear fresh water. Seeker drank from the river and listened intently as the King told him wonderful stories about his Kingdom.

CHAPTER SIX

When Seeker went to bed that night, he was so tired that he immediately fell fast asleep. The rooster had to crow *really* loud the next morning to wake him up. Seeker jumped out of bed, got dressed, ran downstairs, ate his breakfast, and headed toward the door. His mother was standing there like she had the previous morning, smiling and holding his toothbrush. "Oops! Forgot about my teeth again!" Seeker quickly brushed his teeth and then hugged his mother. But today, it wasn't the usual quick hug. Today, Seeker hugged her so hard that she gasped in surprise. "Bye, Mom!" he said with excitement shining from his eyes. "I'm going to see the King!"

"All by yourself," Contentment said with a smile. She waved good-bye and then stood leaning in the doorway, watching her son race toward the Straight and Narrow Path. A deep happiness washed through Contentment's heart as she thought about her son *really* getting to know the King. "I never knew," she whispered to herself, "what contentment really meant...until now."

Seeker reached the path and then came to a screeching halt. To his surprise, all his friends were there. HopeSo, KnowSo, and Yes; Giggles, Gladness, and Glee; Dawdle and Slow; and Doodle and Do stood waiting for him at the big rock. The CARNALville clowns were busily trying to hand out candy and balloons, but the children kept pushing them away. Seeker's friends were acting very strangely; and much to the clowns' dismay, they were singing their song as though they were completely and utterly bored:

> *CARNALville, CARNALville, we love to go,*
> *To the CARNALville, all day long. (SIGH)*
> *Up and down, round and round merrily go around,*
> *We love the Carnival so. (SIGH)*
> *But sometimes those rides make my head hurt and*
> *Sometimes my stomach feels sick;*
> *But the candy tastes dandy—*
> *I don't think there can be*
> *Anything better than it. (SIGH)*

Seeker hurried to his friends and said, "Oh, yes there is! There is some*one* better! The King! He is *much* better! He's wonderful!"

"He is?!" the children asked together.

The clowns frantically offered candy and balloons, desperately trying to distract the children and cover their ears so they wouldn't hear what Seeker was saying. (This was all quite difficult for the clowns to do because they were trembling with fear at the very mention of the King. In fact, they were shaking so badly that they could hardly pick their noses!)

"Yes, the King is wonderful!" Seeker responded with excitement. "I had the best day of my whole life yesterday, and I'm going again today!" Seeker stepped onto the Straight and Narrow Path, then turned back to the children. "Hey, I just got a great idea! Why don't you all come with me to see the King?!"

Quickly, the clowns pushed their way between Seeker and his friends. They offered more candy and balloons. They held out free tickets for the CARNALville rides, but the children ignored them. "To see the King?!" Seeker's friends asked. "You mean, we could?"

"Sure!" he answered. Seeker pushed the clowns back with a strength that surprised everyone, especially himself. The clowns whined and whimpered in pain. Seeker stepped closer to his friends, and then continued soberly, "If you *really* want to! Do you *really* want to?"

The children nodded. "Uh-huh."

Seeker shook his head and folded his arms firmly. "Uh-uh! You must *really* want to! Do you *really* want to? Get that straight 'cause they ask it all the time!"

"Yes!" the children cried.

"The CARNALville just doesn't make me giggle anymore, and Seeker, you look so happy!" Giggles said.

The others agreed. "Yes! We *really* want to get to know the King!"

The clowns had recovered from Seeker's push and now they moved close again. They began to speak in their most candy-coated voices, "Boys and girls, of course you *don't really* want to get to know the King! The King is boring, remember? Come with us. We have more of our very own special secret recipe candy for you!"

"No!" the children cried together. "We don't want any of your candy!"

The clowns pretended to have hurt feelings. "No candy?" they whined. "But it's so good for you! Here, try this piece. It's from our brand new especially most secret recipe." The clowns held out brightly-colored, swirled candy sticks.

Doodle and Do looked at each other. "Do you think we should try one little piece, Doodle?"

42

Dawdle and Slow protectively stepped in front of Doodle and Do and spoke forcefully at the clowns, "D-D-Didn't you hear us or s-s-something? We don't want your candy!"

"But it's very good candy," one clown said sweetly. "Try it." The clown reached out with a stick of candy. Dawdle brushed it aside, and as he did, the edge of the stick caught on the clown's mask and pulled it off.

The children stared in horror at the ugly, slimy, dark face. "Dragon!"

"Seeker was right!" KnowSo cried. "Let's get out of here!"

The dragon-clowns stepped forward again with their candy and balloons. "Wait! Okay, okay, so you found us out. Listen, kids, sure we're dragons, but we're really *nice* dragons! We won't hurt you! Now c'mon and have some candy."

Seeker again pushed the dragon-clowns. This time he pushed so hard that they fell down on the ground, whimpering loudly. All the children looked at Seeker with great respect and admiration. "How did you *do* that?" Doodle asked, as they all walked toward the path.

"I'm not sure," Seeker answered. "But I think it's because I was with the King all day yesterday! And my mom told me about a weapon that..."

"L-L-Look out, Seeker!" Slow cried and pointed behind him. "D-D-Dragons!"

Seeker turned to face the dragons. They had gotten up from the ground, thrown off their clown disguises, and were now rushing toward Seeker in full-force dragon rage. But Seeker wasn't afraid. He remembered the words from the song; he remembered the powerful weapon. He stood very tall and yelled, "In the King's name, you get out of here!"

The effect was amazing. It was like an invisible light-ning bolt had hit the dragons. They flew backwards through the air and landed with a loud thump. They held their bodies and rolled on the ground, screaming with pain.

Seeker grabbed his friends by the hand and whirled back toward the Straight and Narrow Path. "Come on everybody! Let's go!"

"No! *No!*" the clowns shouted, crying out as they tried to get up. "Listen, kids, you can have free lifetime passes to every ride! We'll even give you the recipe for the candy! Come back! Come back!" But none of the children paid attention to the voices of the dragon-clowns. Instead, they all ran toward the castle with Seeker.

The clowns angrily stomped on their balloons, shoved the candy back into their pockets, and picked their noses all the way back to the CARNALville; all the way back to their master in the deep, dark place beneath the trap door of Selfishness.

CHAPTER SEVEN

The Royal Doorkeeper was very surprised to see all the children standing before him at the entrance to the castle. "Who are you?" he asked firmly. "And what do you want?"

"We're the kids!" came the energetic reply. "And we want to see the King!" The children leaned toward the Doorkeeper convincingly. "We *really* want to see the King!"

The Doorkeeper smiled and opened the castle door. "Great! Then come with me!" The Doorkeeper led the children into the castle and down the shining hallway.

When they reached the entrance to the Grand Throne Room, the Doorkeeper slowly opened the huge double doors. He bowed to the King and then stretched out his hand toward the children, motioning for them to enter the Grand Throne Room. The Doorkeeper then stepped back, and the children of the Kingdom went into the presence of the King.

Seeker half-ran and half-slid across the Grand Throne Room floor into the King's great arms. The King lifted Seeker high into the air and twirled him around in circles, laughing. HopeSo, KnowSo, and Yes; Giggles, Gladness, and Glee; Dawdle and Slow; and Doodle and Do watched with open mouths and wonder in their eyes. This was a side of the King they never knew existed.

They watched as the King finally put Seeker back down on the floor and turned his attention toward them. The King smiled at them. It was a very gentle, happy smile. The children smiled back, and then remembered their manners. They knelt down and looked up into the King's eyes. A few moments passed.

"Just say, 'Hi.' " Seeker encouraged his friends.

The children smiled shyly at the King. "Hi," they said.

The King smiled, and responded with a warm, "Hi."

"We're HopeSo, KnowSo, and Yes; Giggles, Gladness, and Glee; Dawdle and Slow; and Doodle and Do," they said softly.

The King bent closer, looked into their eyes, and said just as softly, "I know."

The children looked deep into the King's kind eyes and spoke with all their hearts, "We *really* want to get to know you."

The King bent closer yet and said with all *his* heart, "I know."

Then the King reached out his great hands toward the children and laughed a great laugh. The sound of his laughter echoed past the castle halls, down the hill, and through the streets of Peace and Harmony. Villagers looked up from their work as a delighted shiver briefly overtook them. The King's laughter continued to echo until it reached the CARNALville of Selfishness, where the dragon-clowns shook in violent fear at the sound, and once again felt pain from where the child Seeker had pushed them back with the King's name.

"Come," the King said to the children, "I will show you my castle!"

Getting to know the King was a *great adventure*, and it was just the beginning of wonderful adventures in the Kingdom; but some questions still remain. Why was the King sad? And why is the third banquet table empty?

THINK ABOUT
THE STORY

The best part about this story is that it is *true!*

There truly is a Kingdom of Joy and Peace, and there truly is a King. His name is Jesus. *You* can get to know Him—if you *really* want to.

You can spend time with King Jesus every day. Just whisper His name and He hears you.

TALK TO THE KING

"King Jesus, I don't want to live my life at the CARNALville of Selfishness, trying to always please myself. I want to be like Seeker and *really* get to know You. When You are King and Ruler of my life, it will be a great adventure!"

The people who know their King shall have mega-muscles inside and go on great adventures! Daniel 11:32b *Yeah!*

(Hugga-Wugga™ Paraphrase)

Land of Laws Forgotten

VILLAGE GREED

CARNALVILLE

Valley of Lost Dreams

World Beyond
the Kingdom

Island of
Despair

ROYAL HARBOR

Talking Tree Forest

The Kingdom
of
Joy and Peace

N
E · W
S

The Adventure in the Kingdom™
by Dian Layton

◄── SEEKER'S GREAT ADVENTURE
Seeker and his friends leave the *CARNAL*ville of Selfishness and begin the great adventure of really knowing the King!

◄── RESCUED FROM THE DRAGON
The King needs an army to conquer a very disgusting dragon and rescue the people who live in the Village of Greed.

◄── THE WHITE TOWER
The children of the Kingdom explore the pages of an ancient golden book and step through a most remarkable doorway — into a brand new kind of adventure!

◄── IN SEARCH OF WANDERER
Come aboard the sailing ship, "The Adventurer," and find out how Seeker learns to fight dragons through the window of the Secret Place.

◄── THE DREAMER
Moira, Seeker's older sister, leaves the Kingdom and disappears into the Valley of Lost Dreams. Can Seeker rescue his sister before it's too late?

◄── ARMOR OF LIGHT
In the World Beyond the Kingdom, Seeker must use the King's weapons to fight the dragons Bitterness and Anger to save the life of one young boy.

◄── CARRIERS OF THE KINGDOM
Seeker and his friends discover that the Kingdom is within them! In the Land of Laws Forgotten they meet with Opposition, and the children battle against some very nasty dragons who do not want the people to remember...

Available at your local Christian bookstore.

**For more information and sample chapters,
visit www.reapernet.com**